Patty's PICTURES

Elizabeth Kernan

NEIGHBORHOOD READERS

Rosen Classroom Books & Materials™

New York

I like to take pictures.

This is my house.

This is my school.

This is my park.

This is my store.

This is my bike.

This is my dad.

This is my mom.

This is my sister.

This is my dog.

I like to take pictures of everything!